This book belongs to:

_____

For imaginative people of all ages — T O

Books by Tina Olajide:

Emi's Curly, Coily, Cotton Candy Hair

How Fish Became Stars

This is a first edition published in 2021.

Text copyright © Tina Olajide 2021.

Illustrations copyright © Salomey Adjei-Doku 2021.

A CIP catalogue record for this book is available from the British Library.

ISBN: 979-8-480215-62-5

Emi's DREAMSCAPE

by

TINA OLAJIDE ★ **SALOMEY DOKU**

art by

Based on characters created by Tina Olajide and Courtney Bernard.

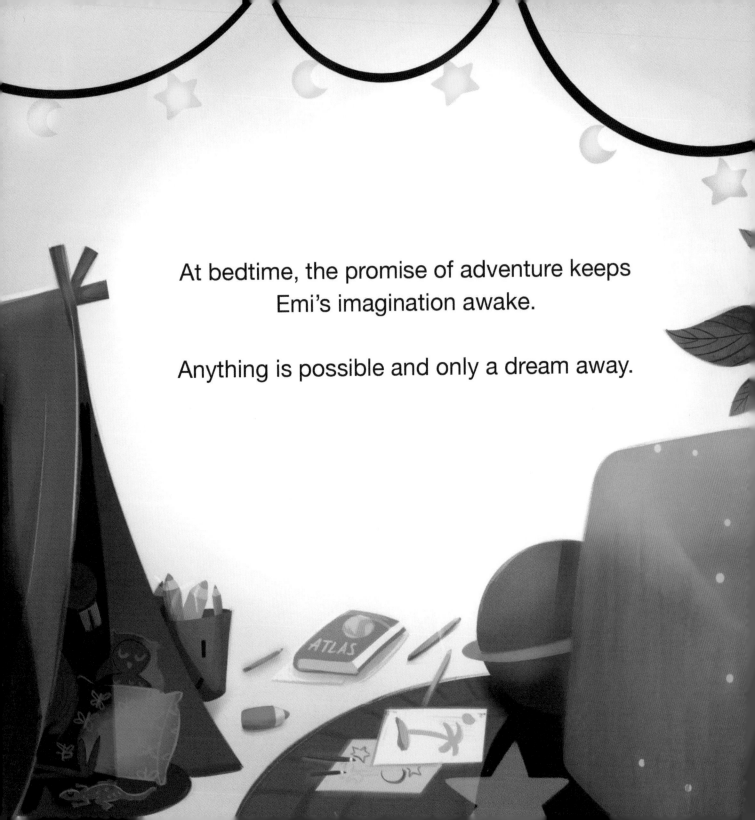

At bedtime, the promise of adventure keeps Emi's imagination awake.

Anything is possible and only a dream away.

In a dark room, a sign points to a quick trip by cosmic slide into the unknown.

Ride the
Cosmic Slide
The fastest way to get
to where you're going!

Emi leans back...

Off she goes! swish, swish, swish,

twisting and turning,

looping

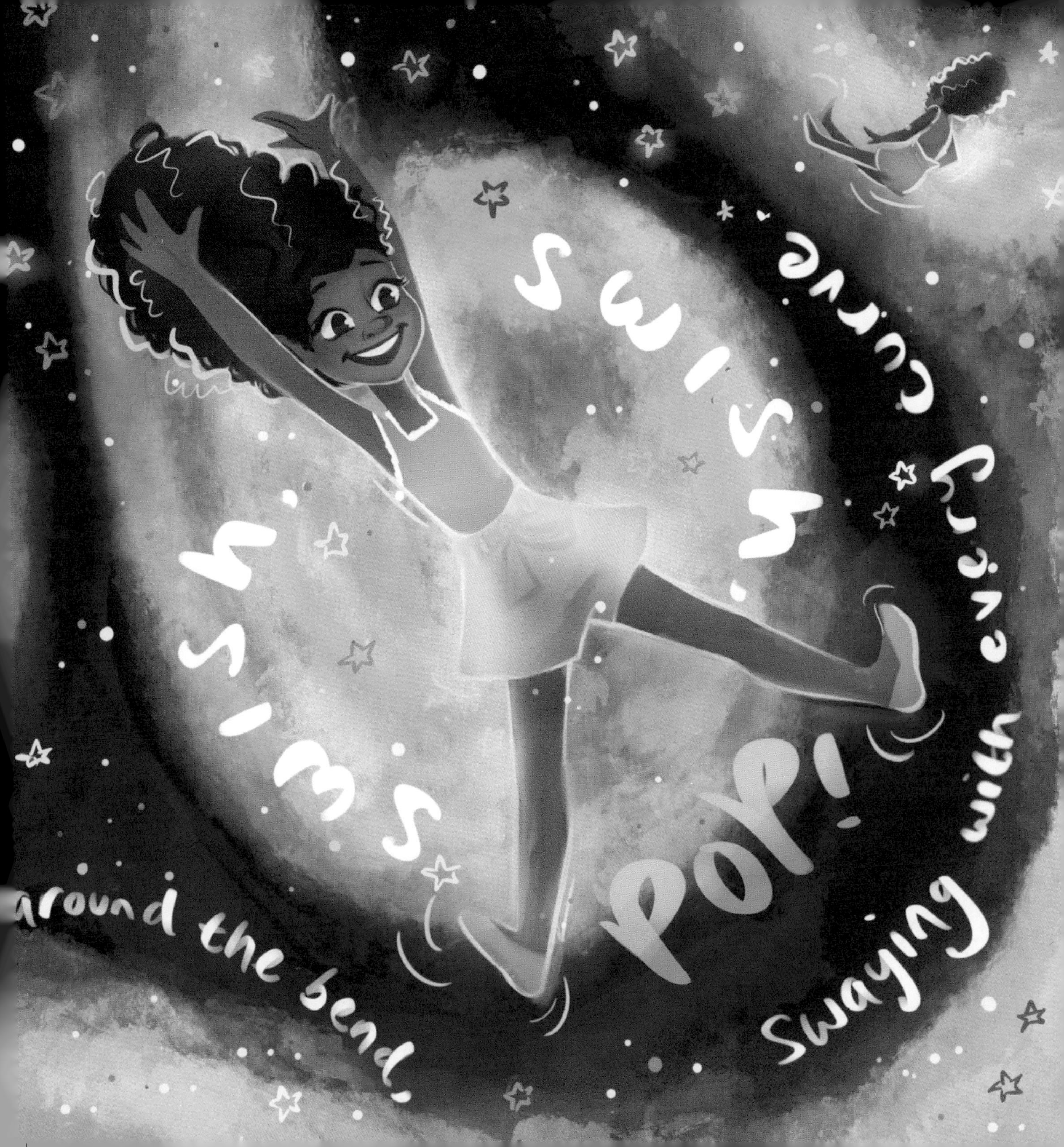
swish
swish
around the bend,
swaying with every curve
pop!

Dizzy, her eyes widen with delight at the sight of so many fish.

A current pulls
Emi away.

She kicks and paddles,
but she's caught in a spiral.

swoosh swoosh swoosh swoosh swoosh

around and around

like a carousel.

The dolphins encircle her,

swimming in the
opposite direction,

to push her up
and out of the water.

...and lands on an enormous leaf —

SPLAT!

She peels herself off
the leaf unharmed.

Walking along the canopy
Emi hears singing.

Three flamingos hum a pleasant tune
gliding through the sky.

A gust of wind shakes the leaves.

Emi misses her step…

Emi just crashed a butterfly dance.

Their wings *fluttering* around the rainforest like *floating* bubbles through the air.

She joins in *skipping, spinning and twirling around* until they reach a flower field.

"Careful, you might get dizzy,"
says a voice.

Emi looks around.

"Up here!"
the voice says.

She tilts her head up to
the sky, a girl waves
from a hot air balloon.

"Hop aboard," she says,
inviting Emi into the basket.

Lavender adds more air to the balloon,
lifting them higher.

The pink and orange sand below
looks like sherbet.

The flamingos join their flock,
singing the same tune from earlier.

Emi and Lavender
land at the base of a mountain.

Lavender gives Emi
a magic flute.

"Play this when
you reach the top,"
she says.

She plays the flute.

It's quiet.

Emi squints at the small bird

far away in the sky.

It gets closer.

That is **NOT**
a small bird.

A starry-faced owl bows.

Emi climbs on its back.

They take off into the sky.

Where will Emi's imagination take her next?

Until then, sweet dreams.

About the Author

Tina Olajide enjoys storytelling. She has sticky notes and notebooks around the house to record ideas that sneak up on her. Sometimes ideas are like a whisper, quiet and swift. Other times they are vivid and resolute. Tina lives in London. Find her at tinaola.com.

More Books by Tina Olajide

Join our reader list at emiandfriends.com

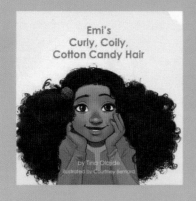

Emi's Curly, Coily, Cotton Candy Hair

by Tina Olajide
Illustrated by Courtney Bernard

Emi's Curly, Coily, Cotton Candy Hair is a self-love story that affirms the beauty of textured hair. It captures the special bond between mother and daughter when caring for Black hair.

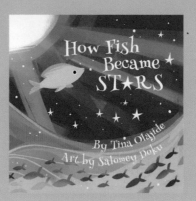

How Fish Became STARS

By Tina Olajide
Art by Salomey Doku

How Fish Became Stars is a heart-warming story about a unique fish, an eventful night and a dream come true. Getting what you want, can show you what you need.

About the Illustrator

Salomey Doku is a bubble tea drinker and nature-lover from Leeds, Yorkshire. She originally trained in architecture - but when a watercolour painting hobby led her on a wild creative journey to freelance illustration, she took a leap of faith and hasn't looked back.

Printed in Great Britain
by Amazon